half MYSTIC

is an internationally-acclaimed independent publishing house, literary journal, radio show, and arts organisation dedicated to the celebration of music in all of its forms. Half Mystic Press, our publishing arm, releases two to four books of prose, poetry, and experimental work per year—invocations of love, wildness, and uncertainty, the heartbeat of humanity set to a 4/4 time signature, expanding and redefining unsung narratives, sharp and lamenting, eyes on the horizon. For more information, books similar to this one, and submission guidelines, please visit www.halfmystic.com.

Praise for *The Family That Carried Their House on Their Backs*

"*The Family that Carried Their House on Their Backs* is a magical story and a family story; its magic evolves from its unfaltering attention to how family—as captivity, as inheritance—can feel. Sammie Downing rediscovers the pure facts of love and and wildness in the spare, strange folklore through which her characters set out. A wise and stunning novella of intense tenderness about the permanence that dwells inside our transience and the wilderness that lives within our homes."

—*Mark Mayer,* author of *The Aerialists,* an *Indie Next* Selection and *Electric Literature* Best Debut

"In this beguiling family romance, a daughter asks her father, 'how do you know what you're looking at in the mirror?' Her question haunts a darkly beautiful fairy tale of a migrant family moving from place to place in an endless wood, told with cheekiness and wit, with a surprise hiding in every exchange between child and parent, human and Wild Thing, house and home. Luxurious and raw, attuned to the wounds in nature that are also wounds in us, Sammie Downing's debut displays an uncanny power, like the family at its center, 'to wring music from your bones.'"

—*Joshua Corey,* Dorset Prize and Fitzpatrick-O'Dinn Award-winning author of *Severance Songs* and *Fourier Series*

"This is one of my favorite pieces ever written. It's as tender as a bruise. It's light and murky and beautiful as nighttime mist descending on a forest. It's whimsical yet slightly acrid. It is courageous and raw and unsentimental. A heartbreaking portrait of sisters and mothers. This story brings me to my knees."

—*Kaisa Cummings,* author of *Home Remedies*

"Mother restarts her memory. Father balances precariously between two worlds. Meanwhile, sisters Miriam and Essie struggle with their parents' sometimes devastating imperfections and what it means to grow up, grow apart, and grow together. In these ghostly bites of prose, Sammie Downing gives us glimpses through windowpanes to the unsettling world of Houses and Hollows, Wild Things and severed keys, and sisters mirrored."

—*Emily Capettini,* author of *Thistle,* winner of the Omnidawn Fabulist Fiction Prize

FIRST PRINTING, DECEMBER 2019
HALF MYSTIC PRESS
www.halfmystic.com

EDITED *by* DANIE SHOKOOHI
DESIGNED *by* TOPAZ WINTERS
COVER ILLUSTRATION *by* JESSIE BROOM

ISBN-13: 978-1-948552-09-7
ISBN-10: 1-948552-09-4

The Family That
Carried Their House
on Their Backs

Sammie Downing

A
Half Mystic Press
Publication

There Once Was a Family

Day by day, Father grew skinnier. His flesh vacuumed his bones, suction creating caverns in his cheeks. His body completed a backward progression. He lost the post-marriage belly, the early twenties pizza-grease cheeks, until he was the shape of an eleven-year-old boy again—awkward and too tall for the span of his arms.

While Mother was away at work, Father caught little Miriam staring in the mirror. Her nose was so close that a foggy wet spot appeared where her breath hit the glass.

"What are you doing, big kid?"

"Trying to figure out what I would have looked like as a caveman."

Father smiled. "Why's that?"

"Because Mother says we were all once cavemen and before that we were monkeys."

Father looked confused but couldn't erase that goofy smile from his face. The smile that made his cheeks appear as they once were—fat and round.

"I used to look like them." Miriam stood on the stool, wearing only Sleeping Beauty underpants.

"That was a long time ago, kiddo. Before there was a Miriam. You weren't ever a caveman."

"How do you know?" Miriam pulled her cheeks apart, making them garishly wide, a contorted primate. "How do you know what you're looking at in the mirror?"

Father stood behind her and turned to face his scruffy complexion. He was quiet for a long time, running his hands along his beard and cheeks. For Miriam, it was like watching a man stare at a ghost—petrified yet unable to tear his gaze away from the skeletal eye-sockets shrouded by thin purple flesh—like bruises so deep they went all the way to the other side. The black hair protruding from his ears in wild tufts. His eyebrows were thicker than they used to be, his nose elongated and flattened by some invisible pressure. Eyes that were once brown had yellowed until they nearly glowed.

"Sometimes I forget I'm a person," said Father. "Then I look in the mirror and I realize this voice, these thoughts, all that shit, is trapped in there." Father let out a growl so low it was almost impossible to hear.

"Don't say shit." But Miriam was already looking for the voice in the mouth of the girl who stared back at her. The voice in her head deserved someone taller and with bigger lips, she decided. She didn't like the body her voice had chosen.

"I could have been a great drummer, you know? Not Buddy Rich good—no one's *that* good—but I could have made a go of it. You know that, kiddo?" Father said to his face in the mirror.

Absentminded, he tugged at the key hanging by his side. Father was never without his key and Miriam often caught him playing with the lanyard stitched to his hip the way she played with her fingernails—bending them back and forth until, eventually, they snapped. But the cord that hung by Father's side would never break. Or at least it wouldn't break so easily. In all the years she'd been alive, she'd never seen it fray.

"Did I tell you that I was in a band when I met your mother?"

"You've told me," Miriam said.

"I did? Well, so long as you know..."

Father let the rest of his sentence go unfinished like the life he presumed he'd left undone. A career as a second-rate Buddy Rich discarded carelessly in a graveyard built from his own choices. And yet, that sentence hung there, incomplete, in Miriam's mind—in the place where thoughts go to ruminate but can never really hide.

So it is when fathers talk to daughters when mothers aren't around.

"Pick up your things before Mother gets home," Father said. Miriam's Barbies littered the dirt floor, naked with tangled, bright pink hair and one rubber heel apiece, slimy with dried bathwater. But Miriam never played with her Barbies. She merely arranged them around House on shelves and windowsills, occasionally adjusting a purse here, a hairdo there.

"I didn't do it," she said, hands on her hips, surveying the mess. This was one of baby Esther's unusual playgrounds.

"Just pick it up, okay?"

Essie liked to carve spaces for herself in the offal and the leftovers. While her sister played in the woods, Essie would sneak into their makeshift Room and secret away the dolls, plucking them one by one from their displays. Essie was as deeply wounded by the sight of those lonely dolls, high on their perches, as if she were the one toyed with but never fully engaged.

Miriam shook her head at the muddy floor of the bathroom. This was just one of her little sister's menageries, containing everything Essie rescued throughout the day: pinecones, cottonwood stars, a rusty jar of glitter. But Miriam knew her sister had collections everywhere, hidden in bushes on the side of House, behind the compost pile among the roly-polys, the hollow of a rotted tree.

Miriam stooped to collect her Barbies, lamenting their chopped hair and Sharpie'd eyeliner.

"I'll make it better," she cooed into the mermaid Barbie's ear. "I'll protect you."

It was the sisters' perpetual game of cat and mouse. Each girl believed she was the only one truly committed to the preservation of the dolls; each was convinced of the other's deeply malicious and destructive nature. It would be several years before the children understood that their desires were, and always would be, the same. Their differences lay not in iterations of destruction but in definitions of preservation. Miriam believed that to be powerful one had to be impervious; Essie believed that nothing was worth having if left untouched.

Later in their lives, men would come to believe themselves in love with one sister until the day they met the other. Upon introductions, they'd think they'd been the victims of a cruel illusion. It was as if one sister passed through an alternate dimension to create the other, leaving mirror images standing on either side of an astronomical cusp. To speak to one was to speak to the other backwards. A pair of lips belonged to her sister, reversed. While one was cool to the touch, the flesh of her counterpart stung an outstretched palm.

So it is with sisters who are spirit twins and total strangers simultaneously.

Scaffolding

Heavy gray envelopes arrived in the mail daily. With every move the Post was delayed by weeks. Sometimes it took months for the mailman to discover the new location of House, but always he found them in the end as he found all Houses. The mailman pushed letters under the canvas door by the handful and before they'd even had a chance to thud to the floor, Father rushed to carry them away to the compost pile, unopened. Envelopes lined the refuse of their dinner in neat little piles—swollen with rainwater.

One morning Miriam found her sister sitting by the compost pile. Flies circled Essie's pigtails and landed on her nose. With the tenderness and precision required for creating new life, Essie plucked the crumbling letters one by one from their piles and rolled them into balls. Big ball, medium ball, tiny head built from wilted paper. Miriam watched as her baby sister made a trail of miniature, rotund paper men that marched away from the rotting food and back towards House again. A hot animal swelled inside Miriam—too large and too angry to be content within such a small space. It beat her from the inside.

"These are Dad's," Miriam said, kicking the little men over. Heads rolled. Bodies spilled across dirt. "Don't be such a baby."

"I'm not a baby," Essie said. "I'm six!" And she held up five fingers in proof.

"You need one more, dumbo."

Essie smiled and lifted another tiny, stubby finger. She was missing her canine tooth; her smile made Miriam's stomach go slack and gooey. Singing to herself, Essie turned to face the massacre of broken paper figures, began collecting the little pieces and putting them together again.

"See? All better. This one is for you." She handed her sister a mushy white ball that weeped blue ink.

Miriam took the sad, sodden torso constructed from Father's secret envelopes and knelt down in the dirt beside her sister.

"I wish you'd beat me up. Or spit on me," Miriam said as she helped Essie pick up the fallen pieces. "Stab me in the eye with a stick or something. Just once, okay?"

"Okay." Essie finished one of her paper men for the second time. Its head was wonky and veered towards the ground. "This one's my favorite."

"Yeah. It's my favorite, too."

꿍

Like envelopes, phone calls arrived with alarming velocity. They had an agreement, Miriam and Father. She would never tell Mother that sometimes Father was already home when she returned from second grade. That Miriam found him in garden—eyes closed, impervious to her words and touch. Miriam would never tell Mother what she saw and in return, Miriam would never have to answer the phone. She could let it ring and ring and ring, let it fill House, never touch it. She hated to answer the phone. There were always men on the other end of the line asking questions about Father and Mother: *whenwilltheybehomesweetie?* and *canyougivethemamessageformeplease?*

Letting the phone ring became Miriam's first experience of ecstasy. She danced in the living room to the sound—the ugliest bird. Laughing, she made up songs to match the rhythm of the ringing. Father was, however unwittingly, teaching Miriam what it felt like to say no— the exalting sensation that accompanied denying someone what he truly wanted. Years later, she would find herself denying, withholding, rebuffing, all the while wondering why it made her feel so electric. Why, when she ignored an expectant touch or an outstretched arm, she had the inane urge to do a little dance.

Father fidgeted his way through dinner, constantly adjusting his shirtsleeve and tugging at the button closest to his neck. He rarely ate, but when he did, it was as if his next meal might never arrive—gorging himself on mashed potatoes until his concave belly protruded, rotund and alarming, from his shrunken frame.

"Slow down," Mother laughed.

Miriam watched Father shovel meatloaf into his mouth and decided that a man doesn't grow that hungry overnight. He acted like an animal deprived. Silent, the family watched Father across the cook-fire outside House. His fingers trembled against the fork as if it were some foreign object he'd long since surpassed.

Miriam had heard of this before—there were whispers at the Gatherings of Fathers or Mothers disappearing in the dead of winter never to return, the sound of howls penetrating the blackness of the woods, eyes that flashed in the night and then went dark as if snuffed out. Everyone knew what happened when you resisted, when you refused to surrender to a life of keys and Houses. The Hollow took what it was owed. You could hide, you could pretend, but the Hollow always knew where you truly belonged. It could sense if you were built for smoke, fire and hearth or if your lungs were sharp with the smell of blood and cold wind through pines. From the Hollow you could never hide.

No matter how far Mother took them, no matter where she moved House, the howls found them once again.

The Hollow was coming to collect.

It was one thing for a little girl to hear talk of Wild Things coming for their brethren, stealing Brothers and Fathers and Mothers from their Houses. It was one thing to hear the whispers of fellow children, the hushed wails of those left behind, and it was another thing entirely to bear witness. A shiver made its slow climb along

Miriam's vertebrae and she pulled her arms closer to her chest. Not for the first time, she wondered why Mother watched but still couldn't see.

After sucking the juice of the meal from his thumbs, Father wiped his hands on his thighs, stood up and walked away without a word.

"Where does he go?" Miriam asked Mother, jumping up but too afraid to follow.

"Nowhere interesting."

The little girl looked from the darkening woods that ringed House and the cook-fire to Mother kneeling by the smoldering logs, loosening the meat stuck to the sides of the pan. There was a heat to Mother's movements. Her hand whisked back and forth over a single spot until the metal shone. If the pot were skin, it would glow red.

❧

One night, long after dishes and girls were both scoured clean, Miriam stood at the edge of her and Essie's little room, waiting. Mother had long since blown out every candle.

House was dark. Wind from the woods made the walls flicker and dance. The breeze carried with it smells of honeyed cedars and ripe rain. Miriam loved House best when the summer wind swept through. No matter where they were, no matter which clearing they'd found, that smell remained the same. Every year, in the season where sunlight stayed longest, Miriam could always count on this wind to return. She took a deep breath that turned to a yawn. Mother and Essie were asleep, but Miriam was good at waiting.

One breath. Two breaths. Ten breaths. The sound of quiet footsteps, and suddenly Father pulled back the curtain. He was home.

There was no light, but it didn't matter—Miriam knew Father just by the way he smelled. His night scent was a mixture of hot breath and coffee, his clothes damp and dusty-sweet. Sometimes she thought Father smelled bad but then she'd sniff each of her armpits and think, *I smell too.* In her mind, her sweat was like the old wet grass piled at the edge of the clearing—earth that never smelled the same way twice.

"What are you doing, big kid?" Father asked.

"I can't sleep."

"Can't sleep, eh?" Father stood in the doorway, waiting. Miriam bit her lip but didn't say anything more. "Okay, let's see what we can do."

They'd always had a seamless bedtime rhythm: Miriam lay down on her belly as Father pulled the blanket up to her waist, making sure to tuck in all the sides, even under her feet. Above them, a summer storm gathered and the wind whipped a quivering House. But not even a thunderstorm could scare Miriam tonight. Father whispered his ancient lullaby into her ear:

eyes burn the tide
water, I beg

find your home and wash these hills clean
my paths are strewn with thorns that bind

As Father sang, he tried to scratch her back the way he used to. But his hands moved frantically over her pyjamas.

"Ouch," Miriam said.

Father sang louder so his voice could be heard over pellets of rain on the tarp:

buckets of paint
men fly, while angels
sink, sink, sink to their knees

The next morning, there were claw marks.

Miriam examined her shoulder blades in the mirror, trying to twist her neck to see herself from behind. She couldn't get more than a tiny glimpse of the red welts before they disappeared from view again. The little girl ended up turning in circles. She laughed. She ran faster.

"Trying to catch your tail?" Mother asked from the door.

Miriam froze, folding her arms across her chest.

"What's this?"

Mother walked closer, ran her fingers along her daughter's spine. Hands darted quick and cold from scratch to scratch, probing for their depth, scanning for bruises. Despite Mother's gentleness, Miriam flinched under the pressure of her searching touch. There seemed to be no end. Sometimes Mother paused, pressed harder over a thick cut. She bent down and laid a kiss between Miriam's shoulder blades. A wet gust of air. A tiny gasp of flesh.

What is it you see? the little girl wondered.

"So, we begin again," Mother said.

"No." Miriam pressed her back against the mirror, trying to hide the marks. "We just got here."

This was her favorite spot, by far. The woods were darker here, the trees so old they started growing short again. Close to a creek, Miriam had taught Essie how to string meat to the end of a long stick and dangle it between the rocks where the water ran fastest. She knew how to lure the crawdads out into light. House wasn't even locked to Mother's back and already Miriam's heart ached for all the bits of wood left unexplored, places along the little river she'd yet to ford.

"That's just not true," Mother said. "We moved under the Bony Moon."

But Mother was wrong and Miriam knew it. They'd arrived just after the long thaw. Grass awoke silver and still but by the end of the day it grew greener, every moment more alive than the one before. Near the creek, daffodils bloomed and baby Essie picked some, making Barbie beds from yellow petals. There had been no winter here, no frozen creek, no House covered in snow.

Miriam stuck out her tongue.

"Wow, what a grown-up," Mother said.

"It won't matter anyway."

Mother ignored her, like Miriam had known she would. There was too much to do now, packing and sorting and arranging, for Miriam's voice to linger in Mother's mind. That was how Mother liked it.

"*I said,* it doesn't even matter if we leave. Did you hear me?"

Miriam looked at Mother's face and saw all the plans and preparations and to-do lists dart through her gaze, flickering in little shadows and bits of light. Thoughts melded with the wrinkled web of Mother's forehead, her eyes. They left a map behind. A map Miriam believed, if only she tried hard enough, if only she paid close enough attention, one day she might learn how to read.

Without warning, Miriam balled up her fists, opened her mouth, and let out a high-pitched scream. Her voice filled House. The sound grew louder and louder until she'd used up every bead of air in her lungs.

"If you're going to scream, go ahead and scream," Mother said calmly. "But if your things aren't ready by lunch, we're leaving without you."

Slip Knot

They came to a vacancy in the woods. Birches parted, revealing a slice of sky and barren earth. It was a good spot —covered in the soft detritus of trees, shielded by leaves from both east and west. But, best of all, it was far from the closest House. Nearby a lone apple tree stood. Come late August the tree would ripen and color the clearing with its sweet, rotten scent.

Mother sighed as twilight surrendered to the first strains of night. Miriam could sense her fear in the tremor of her breath as she lowered to her knees, shifting the clanking behemoth that clung to her thin shoulder blades. The family stood silent in a circle around Mother as her breasts fluttered up and down. House was heavy and Mother was getting older. There were spots of gray now in the hair behind her ears.

The silence of the clearing made Miriam feel like the whole world was about to pop. One minute they'd be standing there and the next, *poof*, the whole family would suddenly burst. She desperately wanted to say something —anything—but even after dozens of moves, she still wasn't sure which words were best.

She should go over to Mother, she thought. Put her hand on Mother's shoulder, wipe the sweat from her cheek. But Miriam wasn't allowed. Watching Mother sit alone in the middle of the clearing, head hanging low, House towering above her in its thick cage, made Miriam's whole body feel heavy. It seemed to the little girl that water had overtaken her, saturated every cell. In order to move, she needed fins, not fingers.

Then, like an invisible current running through live wire, something happened, something Miriam couldn't see. Where just a moment ago there was nothing —only a family standing in the clearing, silent and still— Father suddenly shifted forward as if responding to an inexplicable need. He crossed to Mother's side and tugged at the lanyard stitched into his right hip. There, at the end of the long red cord, hung his key.

Ever since the beginning, Miriam had thought Father's key beautiful. It was so old the metal looked blue instead of silver. She'd been half Essie's age when she'd first seen the key dangling above her, swinging back and forth in a flash of quiet color. She'd grabbed hold and yanked as hard as she could. Father had yelped. *Careful*, he'd told her. *That hurt*.

Now, iridescent under the light of the Moon, the key flickered like some strange insect caught in Father's grip. Mother lifted up her shirt, revealing a little lock hidden within a tiny seam of flesh. Miriam had always marveled at the unassuming hunk of metal embedded within Mother's hip: *Father-holds-key-Mother-holds-lock-lock-holds-House.*

"You ready?" Father asked.

I'm not ready, Miriam thought.

Mother nodded and he slipped the key inside the lock. Mother closed her lips, then her eyes. Held her breath. Miriam knew it had to hurt. The key inside.

Slow, rhythmic clicks from Mother's hip to the top of her spine. With each *ting,* House came further undone. Together the family listened to Mother's body as others might a clock, waiting for the ticks to lead them to a chime. Such a soft noise and yet the unlocking was all they could hear. Louder than the woods in the wind, louder than the crickets—House was louder than it all.

Oh, little family, always waiting for House to fall...

Finally, in a clash of metal, wood and bells, House tumbled to the earth.

Each time Mother and Father set down their home, they moved slower. The act of unlocking and relinquishing House had become such a laborious task that the once-simple process now took close to an hour. Miriam was certain that each of her parents' gestures and sighs contained its own code—that within every ritual, an entire language only her parents understood was both invented and destroyed.

The family stood in front of their House splayed out on the wet leaves. No one spoke. Mother held her hand to her hip, biting her lip. House rippled with the breeze.

"All right, let's get going," Father said.

Young Miriam set baby Essie on the ground to help her parents arrange House. There began a familiar rhythm: Mother and Father rigged tarp and cardboard, hung slivers of glass for windows and scraps of mirror in their bedroom, while Miriam and Essie organized the dishes, arranged their eight books, laid rugs against the warm dirt. In a matter of hours, they'd managed to disassemble and reconfigure an entire exoskeleton of collected fragments amassed over Mother's lifetime.

They heard it as they settled into the darkness and ceremony. Emanating from the depths of the woods, from the Hollow itself, came a throaty howl. The sound grew louder and louder, as if the Wild Thing were crouched at their backs, its breath muggy on the nape of their necks.

And just as the howl had arrived without warning, so it left. In no time, they were alone again in the particular silence of a forest at night.

They finished House quickly, and without a word or a wave goodbye, Father drifted away, off into the space between the trees, as if answering a silent call. Miriam watched the small of his back shrink into nothing but a glimmer of light in the dark wood and fought the urge to run after him, to sit on his feet and clutch his calf the way she'd done when she was little. To become a barnacle that would never let go. *Take me with you,* she wanted to scream. *Come back for me.*

Out of the corner of her eye as Father disappeared into the leaves, Miriam saw Mother flinch almost unnoticeably. As her eyes grew cloudy, Miriam fought the urge to shake her. *Run after him. Fight!*

Instead Mother turned away, rolled out strips of bubble wrap and blankets for Miriam and baby Essie's bed. "This will do nicely."

I told you, Miriam wanted to say. *I told you nothing would be different.* But today was not a day for meanness. That, at least, Miriam knew.

"Yes, it will do nicely," she reassured Mother instead, although she was merely nine years old and had no understanding of what made the perfect place to pitch House. But something in Mother's voice told Miriam what she needed to say. Even then Miriam had a feeling that she would spend the rest of her life repeating her mother's words—to comfort, to calm, to reassure. The line between what Mother needed to hear and what Miriam needed to say blurred until the sense behind her words became difficult for Miriam to decipher. *Yes, this will do nicely.*

To carry a House is a cumbersome trade. It takes strong shoulder blades, a stiff neck and speed. You never know when you might move again.

Dead Load

Mother had to leave them. Their aunt was having her first baby. Housebearers were required to attend new births, Mother explained as she packed her satchel. Before she left she kissed each little girl on their ten fingers and their ten toes and said, "I'll be back."

As soon as she was out of sight, Essie and Miriam flew to the woods, leaping with joy. Mother was the only one who cared about being home before dark, about not climbing too high in trees or keeping away from the creek.

But the further the sisters careened through the woods, the deeper Father crawled into the tattered caverns of House. It was Mother who held Father within his skin; now that she was gone he shivered in his flesh, twitching and clawing at the thick fur that sprouted, fuzzy and tough, from his bare back. Mother's absence: electricity singeing his bones. Molting began.

Deep in the woods the little girls laughed and tossed fallen needles. Sap hung from their hair in matted, syrupy clumps. They acted out ancient myths from a time before Housebearers, taking turns as both princess and dragon.

Then, without warning, their fun turned green. Miriam's face began to sweat and she clutched her belly. Stomach pains roiled in her gut and she lay where she stood, vomiting into the sodden earth. Her brain rolled wild somersaults inside her skull, smashing against its bony walls. She'd never known her body to do anything like this before. She'd never yet rejected herself. Everything Miriam had eaten returned, but it tasted different on the way up—as if her food had passed through the underworld and was rising again from her mouth.

"Miri?" Essie said, touching her sister's shoulder. "Miri, what's wrong?"

But Miriam couldn't answer—she couldn't even breathe. Her heart pulsed loud inside her skin. She felt as though a tight blanket had wrapped itself around her body: stuck and terrified, she couldn't find her way out.

Soon there was no food left inside her, only water. And then there was nothing left at all and yet she still felt her whole body flip itself inside out in an attempt to force her organs past her tongue. She couldn't help it. Miriam began to cry.

Essie licked the tears from her sister's cheeks.

"Go home," Miriam said, tucking her face into the crook of her elbow.

But Essie refused to leave her side. Instead she gathered leaves and petals to make a pillow for Miriam's head until the only thing Miriam could smell was the citrus-tang of pine needles and the green, freshly-living scent of just-cut leaves.

Day turned to night and Miriam lay in a puddle of her own feverish limbs in the woods. As the Moon rose and the temperature dropped, their skin slick and cold, a simultaneous chorus rang in the sisters' heads, their mother's voice: *I'll be back.* Neither slept, only shivered as the howls grew loud around them and the light of the Moon sent tree shadows dancing upon the ground. Even when each girl cried out in fear, Father did not come.

Essie stroked her sister's face with pudgy fingers, ignoring the sticky vomit on Miriam's chin, the sheen of sweat on her brow.

"I'm going to die," Miriam whispered. She had only a limited idea of death, but her mouth was dry and tasted of bile and bits of her Mother's meatloaf. She could taste herself, the sweaty, desiccated savor of her own tongue.

"Not if the fairies get you first," Essie said.

"There's no such thing as fairies," Miriam said, sucking in her cheeks, trying to hold her stomach inside.

"You know that's not true," Essie said. It was hard to tell if her tender smile was illuminated by the ghostly silver rays of Moonlight, or if it was a beacon lit from somewhere within. Essie bore her own light.

The whole world spun. Miriam thought she saw the trees around them light on fire, but as soon as she blinked they were dark again.

"Why are you such a baby? You make me sick."

Essie leaned down and kissed Miriam's cheek, her lips hot and fat against her sister's clammy skin.

"Don't touch me."

"Okay." But Essie scooted closer instead.

"Why don't you just go away and never come back?"

Essie tucked her body so tightly beside Miriam's that they morphed into a Russian doll: not two sisters but a singular creation containing secret sheaves. In order to reveal each layer you'd have to pluck them apart.

It was so dark that there was no light to eat noise. Sounds roamed free. Every rustle grew louder and louder, until Miriam thought her eardrums might shatter with the smallest tremble of a branch or the flap of massive wings pumping against blackness. It was because of the dark that Miriam could hear her sister's heartbeat, calm and solid, bleeding steadily into the air around them. One beat followed the next with such assurance that Miriam felt herself growing confident again. *If our bodies know where to take us, why not follow?* Essie was warm and soft against Miriam's body, a cloud of heat and baby fat. She smelled sweet, like a cob of corn.

"I hate you," Miriam said.

"Okay."

"You must be deaf. I said I hate you."

Essie snuggled closer and turned her head to face her sister. They were nose to nose. Their breath became a fog between them, revealing their faces and shrouding everything else.

"Okay."

"I'm the big kid, remember?"

This is what you would have heard if you'd been there in the woods that night. But what was really said between the two sisters was larger than any weight a human tongue could bear. Long ago they'd decided that speech was a blunt object, and what they required instead was a silver boning knife—bold and bloody—able to extract the elegant skeleton that held their worlds together without inflicting any damage. Somehow Essie knew Miriam's mind even if Miriam only ever said the opposite. They lived in their own universe where neither sister ever had to say *don't leave me,* or *I'll always be there for you,* or *I wish everything were different,* or *I'm so scared I can't breathe.*

Miriam put her arms around her sister's chest, pulled her tighter. Essie was so soft. She was so small. Those things weren't supposed to make you stronger, but when Miriam felt the pillow of Essie's body against her own, her baby sister's fat fingers holding hers, the sounds of the dark hunting birds swooping in the grass around them became the sound of fairies taking flight—leaping from their bowers and soaring towards the Moon.

As she fell asleep Miriam thought: *if I die, I won't remember being alive. I won't remember lying on the floor of a world where there was no up or down and I could pretend I stretched on and on for infinity. I won't remember that once, it was just me and Essie alone in the dark.* And that is what made her sad. That is what made her lonely.

᠀

In the morning Miriam discovered she could walk if she held her sister's hand.

One foot in front of the other, two little girls made their way from the woods to a House in the center of a bright clearing.

They found Father in his bedroom. Smoke pooled from the twisted curl of his mouth. His eyes stared out blankly. There was no Miriam and no Essie. There was only a place beyond.

Some things Miriam would carry with her forever, and Father's eyes on that day—those yellow orbs staring straight through her—would become intrepid stowaways. Some days she'd open her pocket to find them staring up at her from the bottom, flecked with lint. Other times she would be walking barefoot in the woods and look down at the mud squelching between her toes, and there they'd be: Father's blank, dry eyeballs, lolling among the muck. No matter how many times she threw them in the river, sliced them open with her knife and served them to the foxes, or smashed them flat between a mortar and pestle—Father's eyes would roll back to her again.

"I'm dying," Miriam said now. *Please look at me.*

Father began to sing to himself and for a moment Miriam believed he saw them, that he was lulling them to sleep the way he used to. That he was telling her it was going to be okay.

find us a shore, bring us new sky

25

my soul be bound in darkness
'cross oceans and moors,
wherever there is life, crawl your way forward

Through the fog and stink, Father's song felt tender and forgiving. Miriam reached out to touch him, if only to let him know she was there—*yes, yes, I do still love you*—but when her hand neared his, Father snapped at her fingers with his brown teeth.

"Ouch."

Miriam coiled herself tighter. Curled into a ball, puked what was left to puke, held Essie's hand.

As the girls fell asleep at their father's feet, Miriam marveled that even the young can die.

❧

But Miriam didn't die. Instead Mother returned to find them exactly where they lay. She pulled back the curtain and took in a giant's breath. It sounded as if she had sucked all the air from House, from the woods, from the Hollow beyond, deep into her lungs. All that air made a balloon of her body: as if it were possible for one person to breathe long and hard enough to float away.

Without speaking, Mother carried Miriam to the bath. Wiped the crusted vomit from Miriam's lips.

"From here on out, Memory begins," she whispered.

Cross-Stitch

As the rocks below the earth released their moisture in a fog, Father snuck to the garden. They'd moved House and yet things hadn't changed. Through the window Miriam watched as Father tore the earth with a metal spade, ripping little holes into the ground. In angry flurries he flung dirt across the clearing. The glint of lavender Moonlight on metal ricocheted outward. Quietly Miriam slipped downstairs, through the door of House, and into the growing darkness of the night, dragging Goodnight Bunny through the dirt behind her.

Miriam climbed high into the branches of the apple tree, a perch from which she could observe Father undisturbed. In House, Miriam was just a girl whose parents tucked her between raggedy sheets. Spying on Father from the window made her feel small, caught in a role she didn't belong. But in the garden Miriam was the master of fools, a sprite awaiting mischief. Out here, she was free to see.

Oh, little girl, watching Father from between the leaves...

It was about time for the apples to fall; their overripe smell weighed heavy on the warm night air.

Mother was outside House, by the cook-fire washing dishes, unaware of Father's angry hole-digging or the way his stringy hair concealed hollow, hazel eyes. He'd been wearing the same suit and tie for three weeks now. Between holes Father let out angry coughs, like the chuffs of a great, starving beast.

After she'd washed the dishes, late enough that she was sure the children were safely asleep, this is where Mother found him—walking back and forth examining his haphazard holes, making worry lines in the soil as he stomped the baby heads of squash.

Mother rubbed her temple. Things were disappearing. Today it was her ring; last week it had been her grandmother's sapphire necklace; last month, Miriam's guitar.

Miriam, concealed in the darkness and the smell of rotten apples, watched as Mother shook her head back and forth.

"Maybe we're both losing our minds," Mother said. Father made no reply. Her house-heavy shoulders sagged as she waited at the edge of the clearing.

Mother often waited like this for Father to come home, or to leave his smoky orb that smelled of plastic and epoxy. Miriam called it Mother's waiting stance: one arm curled over her breasts and onto her shoulder, fingers kneading the flesh between her neck and arm. In the evening light, the lines on Mother's face looked like silver thread. For a moment Miriam was frightened that Mother had turned to stone while she wasn't looking.

"So, we begin again," Mother murmured as she turned and walked back into House.

Finished with his holes, Father sat back in the mud with a sigh. His skin glistened white in the coming dark. He looked up with thick, leaden eyes, eyes that saw nothing, and stared blankly at Miriam dangling from a branch. Was it just her or were Father's eyes narrower than before, his chin longer, face slender and determined? Did his lip twitch in a fleshy snarl?

Maybe they were all losing their minds.

A lonely howl reverberated throughout the clearing. The sound came from the Hollow and to the Hollow it returned, a sonic boomerang. Father's ears stiffened as he turned away from Miriam, sniffed the air around him. Terrified of premonitions and portents, Miriam dropped from the tree and ran from the howls, from her Father lost to his smoke and his space, and went to check on Mother instead.

For many years Miriam had believed that Mothers try to drown themselves when their children are not watching. Only later would she realize that not all mothers—just hers—want to throw their bodies away with the bath water.

They always built the bathtub before they built anything else for House. Each new House site began with Miriam and Mother on their hands and knees digging a cavity in the earth—lining the dirt with only the smoothest stones. Every night, Mother heated kettle after kettle on the dying embers until she'd filled the earthen cavern with water and steam. By morning all the water had disappeared through the cracks between stones.

In the candlelight and bathwater, Mother's breasts floated like the pale heads of octopi. Miriam knew, even then, that one day she would have breasts too, and that someone would find them beautiful. But now she was repulsed. Repulsed by womanhood, by roundness, by hips that could carry things within them, by hair covering thick, purple lips below. She was still a girl who believed she was really half-boy-half-water-nymph, and no one yet wanted her for anything more than her energy and her skill of building fortresses out of sticks. She did not know yet that this was a time that would end.

"I will never grow hair on my belly, or my toes," Miriam informed Mother from the door. She said it like she believed it. Like she'd never wanted anything more in her little life. And then, eyeing her mother's white stomach beneath the water: "I will never grow so sad that I want to eat the whole world."

"Whatever you say, sweetheart." Mother dipped her head below the water and Miriam waited to make sure Mother resurfaced. She wouldn't leave until she saw her Mother breathe.

Lateral Force

The next night Essie's Barbie dolls went missing, and she ran to Miriam's corner to discover that her sister's too were gone. Every one of them, vanished, and their little dresses, too. At first Essie thought Miriam had broken the rules of their game—a cardinal, sisterly betrayal. And oh, how Miriam would've loved to be a bandit caught red-handed, to proclaim proudly that it was she who'd whisked the dolls away like a thief in the night.

But Miriam was never a good liar.

"From here on out, Memory begins," Mother said when she saw them there, together at the window.

Essie cried for her babies, and for every tear she shed, one of Miriam's was locked away forever. The little girl tucked her head into the eave of her sister's shoulder, letting out great slurps of tears. As Miriam wiped sweat-soaked hair from her sister's cheeks, she cleared her throat. "There once was a family..."

Essie's forehead was warm against her chest.

"There once was a family that carried their house on their backs."

As Miriam spoke, she thought: *I will churn the truth for you. I will digest its fibers, suck on its sinews,*

31

salivate on its hardness and its shell. I will regurgitate for you, baby bird. Make it palatable. I will do this for you now. But by the end, it will be you who will show me how to see in the dark. It will be you who gives me the strength to believe in things I have never seen.

So it is with sisters who inhabit their own constellation. One always rising, the other falling, never level and never apart.

"There once was a family. Don't be afraid."

Oh, the lies that sisters tell...

Chain Stitch

Miriam finally understood: it was madness to keep such a Wild Thing, selfish and cruel. Houses burn Wild Things. That is why, in the middle of the night, labradors and poodles become coyotes and wolves, their scowling voices reverberating through the neighborhood. When a cat drags mice to the door or slinks to the window with a dead frog in its jaw, we say—*how horrid, how evil, how cruel*. But the cat says *this House, these dishes, this pattern— how horrid, how evil, how cruel*.

Father was like all Wild Things: he could no longer handle the sting of wooden floorboards on his bare paws, the swishing sound of Mother adjusting the lanyard at his hip. Only he could hear the sound of the key turning in the lock. The noise scraped against his eardrums.

After midnight, Miriam watched from the window as Father snuck back to the garden and planted little velvet bags in the holes he had made in the earth. Fog rose up and swirled around him, obscuring his legs and hands, sometimes swallowing his figure entirely. The Moon was full; its face illuminated the garden with an eerie silver glow. The light made everything from the apple tree to Father's emaciated body dead and waxen. His entire body grew thick with black hair that stood on end, as if electrified on his spine. Father's Moon-shadow arched across the garden, a dark, elongated hunchback stalking the perimeter. He tucked each bag into the earth with a gentle pat. As she observed the ravaged form of Father pacing beneath the milky light of the Moon, Miriam began to understand that cognizance was a weight you could never shake.

When he had finally slunk back into the house, Miriam went barefoot to the garden, dragging Goodnight Bunny behind her. She hesitated at the border, looking into the tangled nest of vegetables and weeds.

Digging through the earth for Father's hidden pouches was a clandestine project. She knew what Mother did not: Father was not mad but an animal. A wily wolf, a trickster, a Wild Thing with subterranean caches. But sometimes even animals are afraid of being so very Wild. And Father wanted to be crazy. He desperately wished he was unfit, unequipped for his obligations. Then it wouldn't be called running away. Then he wouldn't have to accept that at one point he had had a choice, Housebearer or Wild Thing, and that he'd chosen wrong. That his life was a lie.

Poor Mother just needed Father to be lost. She wanted him to be wandering, in need of only a flashlight in the dark. A temporary issue, like cold feet before their wedding night.

But it was simpler and more complicated than all that, and only Miriam knew it. This Father, the one with yellow and red eyes, was a Wild Thing. He bit at tethers, lived through insatiable hunger; he was a creature with hidden stores and shiny hoards.

It was easy to find the purple pouches below the surface of the earth. With a tiny intake of breath, she opened the first bag. Yellow receipts unfurled through the opening.

1. Diamond ring
2. Gold necklace, sapphire pendant
3. Guitar, conn
4. Star Wars: Episode III, artifact

Miriam tucked the little slips back below the ground, wishing these thin yellow pages could sprout into many-layered onions with purple stalks. That nourishment could grow from what had been stolen.

She remained in the garden the whole night, looking through the ruin of Father's holes until she fell asleep. She refused to return to her bed, pretending instead that she was a Dryad metamorphosed. She dreamed she'd become one with bark and leaf.

Only with the dawn did Mother come looking for her little girl. It seemed to Miriam, in the blinding light of day, that Mother looked different. A part of Miriam believed that now she knew Father's secret Mother might never look the same to her again. As Mother approached her she thought she could catch—what? A hint of jealousy? Or was her expression simply a trick of the sun?

Though each could only partially explain why, in that moment both women and girl felt untenably betrayed. Mother wounded by Miriam's refusal to give in to the story, the mythos with which she continued to build her house. Betrayed by her daughter's stubborn insistence upon unearthing what she'd given her life to entomb. An occupation so consuming that Mother rewired even the mechanics of her memories, allowing her nightly dreams to cyclically dispose of anything that did not agree with the narrative she'd chosen.

Every morning, Mother began again.

Meanwhile Miriam glanced between her Mother's haggard eyes and the fecund holes, betrayed by her Mother's love. By the lengths the woman went to make love stay.

With and Against the Grain

"Come," Mother said, and waited for the little girl to disentangle herself from the branches and decaying fruit.

Inside House, a sewing kit lay by the bath. The package was complete with the requisite notions: pushpins, needles rusted from centuries of use, scraps of fabric, crimson thread, a hunting knife and iron lock. Miriam trembled at the sight of it placed so unassumingly before her, and Mother rested a soothing hand upon the little girl's back.

"It's time," she said, and gestured for the child to seat herself on the wooden chair next to the bath, its arms forming a fence around her body.

Miriam looked up into her mother's quiet, longing eyes and saw in them something that terrified her beyond understanding: Mother wanted her to build a better House. To grow up, Miriam must be initiated into this world of wire, thread, scraps of metal and photographs—the physical accouterments of a well-intentioned life. But Miriam knew it wasn't so simple as that. To grow up the way her mother wanted, she must accept the woman's sadness, that gaze, that unfinished life, as her own.

And yet—if she said No?

Miriam tried to imagine what it would be like to slowly become a Wild Thing. It might take years before she drifted, the way it had with Father. But if she rejected her House, her tribe, eventually her body would lose its ability to bear a house. She'd slip into Wildness. She'd belong to a feral world devoid of language and tribe—a place where there was no baby Essie, no Mother—where the possibility of motherhood didn't exist. The inevitability sickened her. She thought about standing at the edge of the woods, listening to the calls of the Wild Things, the way their howls surged into the fabric of her flesh, ricocheted in her marrow, set fire to all her places that had no names. She thought about the exhilaration in the pit of her gut when she rejected someone's deepest desire. She thought about how, in the end, she understood what even Father didn't—that the choice was simple. All you had to do was say Yes.

What could Miriam do besides make Mother happy? It was so simple, the act of threading familial and ancestral history—time—into her sinews and cords. How could she refute such a physical tradition? How could she deny her own body from the body that created it? Was it possible to relinquish her tribe before she'd ever truly belonged to one? *What does it mean to choose a life?*

Before Miriam, Mother curled her arms around her body, afraid to consume space, as if she had to ask permission to occupy air that did not expressly belong to her. They were alone in the room, Mother with her wet, melancholy eyes and Miriam, already cold, already hard and unyielding.

If Miriam didn't take this thread, this node with which her future was to begin, she'd be telling her mother, *I don't want what you have*. Or, *you've wasted your choice*. Or, *I don't want to build this better. I don't want to build it at all*.

What does it mean to make your Mother happy? What does it mean when, despite everything, you still want to make your Mother happy?

Perhaps there was still time, she thought, wild and desperate. Perhaps what was done now could be undone, whorled backwards later in life, a spool unwound to infinity. Perhaps one day she could rewind this moment to the beginning of time—all the mothers, grandmothers, great grandmothers bringing their daughters a first kit. All of those women saying: *you belong to us*.

Perhaps it was possible for Miriam to dismantle it all, until the day, in an alternate world exactly like their own, Mother would stand over another Miriam, beside another Father, and she would be happy.

What Miriam wanted beyond anything else was the possibility of containing more than two diametrically opposed choices within herself. She wanted to live a life outside of binary rules. Not only that—she wanted to recode all Housebearers, her mother, baby Essie. Miriam wanted to rip lanyards from hips, locks from flesh. She wanted to live in the time of cavemen, before there were Housebearers or Wild Things.

But didn't simply possessing that desire, that craven fight like a heartbeat, mean she'd already chosen? Was it too late for her already?

And so, like Mother, like all Mothers before, Miriam fell victim to the greatest fallacy of all: that there is still time, any other time but now.

Tears in her eyes, fingers trembling as she gripped the knife, Miriam pierced the flesh at her hip. Blood dotted her skin as she peeled it apart. *What does it mean to choose a life?*

"That's it," Mother said. "It will only hurt for a minute."

Dry Rot

After Miriam tucked Essie into bed that night, the wound from her new home still fresh and stinging, she crept to her parents' door, waited for their night voices to subside. When Father's snores began to slink through the hallway the little girl walked into their room.

There is nothing so secret as watching your parents while they sleep. It takes advantage of their childness, the littleness of themselves they keep hidden during the day. Inside the sheets everyone appears small again. It could all be just a game.

She walked over to Father's side of the bed. More Wild Thing than Father now, Miriam watched as he curled around Mother, his pink paws on her waist, the fur on his back ruffling with every snore. Miriam wondered, not for the last time, how her Mother couldn't see, why she wouldn't ever see. How could Mother bring herself to fall asleep each night in the clutches of a Wild Thing?

The little girl quietly raised his nightshirt over his hip, where the lanyard and keys were stitched. She positioned the scissors over the seams and began to snip each thread. Blood leaked from the seams but Father only grunted, didn't wake up. With each *snip* the keys came further undone.

Wiping blood from her hands, Miriam put down the scissors and carefully placed a Band-Aid over the hole the keys had left behind. Before she crawled from the room with the keys and scissors, she left Father with an Eskimo kiss.

Poor Mother, the girl thought—to wake up without her Wild Thing, only an empty House hiding in bed beside her.

Bind Off

Father found his way to the Hollow like melted snow to the river. After his daughter snipped him free from the House that had stymied him all these years, he meandered, weightless, through the remnants of his world. Houses looked different through his wolf eyes. Paths that had once been so familiar became cement wilderness. Occasionally the wolf stopped to scratch his shoulder blades in places he could never reach before. The scratching sent shivers of satisfaction down his bony spine. He'd never realized it was possible for a piece of your body to forget what it felt like to be touched.

Paws against earth felt different than feet against socks against shoes. Father pissed on Houses, toyed with sticks between his brown teeth and wet black gums. Once, the sight of a swing he'd pushed Miriam on as a child nearly startled him out of his wild fur. He paused a moment at the black, plastic crescent swaying beneath transparent hands. It took great strength to contain that human quiver in his lungs—that two fisted chokehold on his heart.

Father couldn't remember much of the night before but he could just barely recall the pressure of a little girl's fingers against his side, the feel of a child's nose brushing against his. Now, despite the weightless sensation that flooded his every limb, Father's nose stung. Whatever they'd had before last night, Miriam had let him go. He knew it in his bones. She'd cut him free.

So Father padded onward.

Directionless, the wolf moved instinctively to the place all Wild Things belong: the Hollow. Once a natural delta, a receptacle for spare water, but now an asylum for unwanted parts and refuse. No parent let their child play in that green chasm in the heart of the woods. There the trash of a thousand years lay discarded and overgrown. Televisions, fuzzy with lichen and red with rust, stood on end like tombstones. Shards of amber beer bottles blended in with mushrooms. Electrical cords masqueraded as copperheads; cardinals flashed through the surrounding trees in crimson sparks.

Father felt the moss against his claws. He loved how he made no sound as he moved. The stream in the Hollow glistened with a purple and blue graphite sheen; little rivulets made their way inwards, twisting and braiding until they hit the center, and when Father peered into the water he became a metallic Narcissus. Littered with wolves, the Hollow released the pungent smell of half-rotted meat, salt from sweat and bruised fruits. And yet, sprinkled through the organic grime was the smell of lilacs, day lilies, an indescribable iris perfume.

The Wild Thing did not say hello when he arrived but even so his friends howled a chorus of welcome. He shook the dew off his coat, splattering the snouts of his neighbors, and settled in to quietly lick his poorly stitched wound.

Little girl, he thought—losing her name in the smell and noise of the Hollow—she was never good at sewing.

Weephole

But what happens when there are no more Wild Things left to scold, to hold?

The morning after Miriam set Father free, Mother woke to nothing but an empty House in bed beside her. She turned to face the window. Allowed herself one moment of ignorance, one moment devoted to that guttural, childish craving for a time machine. A mulligan. A do-over. A new life. A shade of yearning she hadn't experienced for many years, grown dormant and crusted with nostalgia. After a deep breath, Mother buried her feet in brown slippers and her hands in the pockets of her black robe.

Mother's House had performed mitosis for years now. From its origins as a simple photograph stitched into the lining of a dress, to a small neat package resting on her shoulders, to a massive conglomerate of boxes and packing tape sewn like a bridge between man and woman. It was too large now to be broken down easily. All that growth, and still one morning she'd awoken to find nothing but three drops of blood lying in bed beside her.

"From here on out, Memory begins."

It was the transitory time right before the sun rose, when House was at its coldest. Mother walked outside to the cook-fire and placed a coffee pot over the embers.

Soon after, Miriam and Essie ran outside and sat on the logs beside the fire, swinging their legs back and forth, giggling, impatient for their French toast. Their mother stood above them, hovering over the flames. Miriam always loved to look at the eggs whipped in the blue bowl. The liquid floated serenely before Mother placed the bread inside. The soft yellow juice was speckled with cinnamon and nutmeg, like a fairytale eggshell.

Mother was always soft. She tenderly plucked a slice of bread with slender, piano fingers, slipped it into the batter, dipping both sides, and then flipped it onto the pan to sizzle. The air smelled like morning: smoke, syrup, cinnamon and Mother's coffee.

When all was finished, Mother passed each little girl a plate and sat down beside them, in front of the fire. Essie poked Miriam in the thigh.

"Ow."

"Tee hee, tee hee."

Strawberries were neatly sliced and arranged on a cerulean blue platter. As they began eating, the flames flickered without being stoked.

"Girls," their mother began, eyes on her mug. "We're going to move in with Grandmother for a while."

"Yay!" Essie cried. She loved Grandmother's Barbie collection. After a day spent in Grandmother's House, headless Barbies littered the floor.

Their Mother began to cry. Miriam leaned over and stroked her cheek.

"Don't touch me."

"Okay." Miriam pulled her hand away.

"I said, don't touch me."

"Okay." Miriam's hands were in her lap.

"Damnit, Miriam, I said *don't touch me!*" Suddenly the coffee was soaking into the dirt as Mother began to slap the little girl. Hitting her face, her flat chest.

"Don't touch me!" Mother's thumbs pressed into Miriam's arms as she shook Miriam. Essie was crying.

"Okay, Mama. Okay." Miriam's hands were behind her back, useless against the blows.

"Don't ever touch me like that again!" Mother pushed her down. As she fell, Miriam hit her head on the stones that lined the cook-fire, dangerously close to the simmering embers. Head met rock—*crack*—the sound of an eggshell breaking in half.

The world flickered in sparks and fireworks around Miriam. She saw everything in pieces—the golden morning mist, her mother's tender hair, the glow of Essie's cheeks. The heat of the embers was bright against her face. She wanted to fall asleep forever but instead she slowly stood up.

Mother had collapsed on the ground, her head in her hands and her knees to her chest. Without speaking,

Miriam stood over her and watched her chest rise and fall. The little girl counted to ten before she knelt beside Mother, reached out with the sleeve of her pink robe to wipe the side of Mother's wet cheek.

"Go ahead, call somebody," Mother said into her folded arms. "Tell them. Tell them I can't do this. Tell them to take you away from me."

"Okay, Mama. It's okay." Miriam curled up next to Mother, shaking on the ground. "Come here," she whispered, and Essie snuggled into her lap, the littlest spoon.

❧

The next day, when Miriam stepped out of the bath, Mother was waiting for her. She toweled off the little girl, stroking each limb with ticklish fabric. She paused at a blue bruise on Miriam's arm. "Where'd you get this, little duck?"

Miriam looked from the purple blot to Mother's puzzled look.

"Dunno."

"Be careful, honey," Mother said, and kissed the little girl's nose.

Inside Miriam, a tiny sea broke free.

The Wolf

All animals sprout pigeon brains at the sight of food. Cerebral caps shrink like de-shelled walnuts when smells waft in. It was almost 11 P.M. in the Hollow, and the wolves descended in a deluge of fur, down the hillside to the muddy stream at the bottom.

Each starving wolf for himself. They pawed at the ground, splashing mud onto their hides. Their ears twitched at the simplest sounds—birds shuffling across the branches, squirrels snapping nuts in two. Father avoided standing too close to the others, pacing between the pack and the woods.

They stood and waited until their collective eardrum registered the sound of a hoof sliding against leaves. At that the pack seethed forward, Father close behind. Nipping above the deer's ankles, the wolves slowed the creature down bite by bite. When it was fully encircled—antlers bowed in towards its head—Father fidgeted back and forth between two other wolves. The deer reeked.

Animals do not care about killing; they care about eating. You would too, they say, if you could hold pennies between your ribs as you walked. So when the deer finally fell, half its side in pieces on the ground already, the wolves plunged into the animal out of fear rather than desire. Each wolf's hunger became a tangible ghost at his side, egging him forward, pushing the other animals aside. *Keep going, it's a lonely world,* the hunger said. *Keep going, keep the others out!*

Father hid from the teeth, the snapping, the pushing. Ate only the ankle of the deer.

To Darn

Today they set House down again, minus one. Mother turned to each little girl, touched their shoulders like sheets and said, "from here on out, Memory begins."

Grandmother let them start again, with her this time. Grandfather had died years ago, Miriam knew, and the old woman was lonely in her house by the lake. Once as small as their own House, Grandmother's had grown colossal with each passing year. Now it was as wide as her life—built of the blankets her daughters had slept in, wood Grandfather had chopped when he was still young enough to wield an axe, walls of blue bottles she'd found in the gully when Miriam's aunts were still babies. As the little girl walked through the House, she could run her fingers along Grandmother's memories, hold Mother's childhood in her hands.

Without Father's key, Mother couldn't remove the inanimate creature from her shoulders. It was fused to her body forever. But she could lift pieces of it away—a box here, a box there—removing everything that was important, leaving only the superfluous. Sleep was harder for her now. House weighed heavy on her. Once Mother was in bed, it was hard to move.

Mother's Memory had restarted 3,650 times; it was beginning to show signs of strain. When you carry your House with you over many years, it isn't long before you start leaving things behind. It starts with the rug your aunt gave you, then your Tuscan stoneware, until even memories are lost in the shuffle. Mother, however, had left them behind on purpose. Memories weren't lost but abandoned. Sloughed into dust. If something went missing, it wasn't forgotten—it never existed.

Mother squeezed her shoulders to get rid of the inner itch. "So, we begin again."

Today their grandmother watched the whole business while drinking a Corona, keeping her windy words to herself.

The girls slipped their puzzle piece bodies into the empty spaces of Grandmother's House as their mother wiped her hands on her jeans and left them to dream.

❧

After Mother tucked the girls in for the night, she and Grandmother sat by the lake with their embroidery and gimlets. Miriam, never asleep when she should be, stood at the window, watching them crouched at the edge of the water.

For a long time the two women sat in silence, each perfecting their tiny stitches. Mosquitos flitted at the edge of the light, frightened of the burning citronella candles.

"Do you remember," Grandmother said finally, "when you were little and you watched the tomatoes in the garden? Do you remember how sad you were when I'd pick only some and leave the others behind? You were so worried those forgotten tomatoes would be lonely. So scared those little things would feel abandoned. And nothing I said could change your mind. So you'd run out in the middle of the night and pick the remaining tomatoes, still green, and bring them on home."

"Look, Mom, I appreciate what you're doing for us," Mother said.

"I know, I know. You don't want to hear it."

"I'm just not in the mood right now, Mom. Can't we sit and be quiet?"

"For once in your life, just listen to me." Grandmother reached out and put a hand on her daughter's cheek. "Some things have to be left behind, Penelope. It's the only way they can grow."

"Mom, I told you, this is just temporary. The girls and me, we're going to get back out there on our own.

"That is not what I'm saying, and you know it. Stay as long as you want. Just remember, a Wild Thing is always going to find a way to weasel on back. You have to be tough."

Mother pricked her finger with the needle and Miriam watched as she put her finger to her lips, sucking out the blood before it left a stain. "It's just childish, what he did. That's all," she said. "Children aren't dangerous, they just don't understand. You've got nothing to worry about, all right?"

Grandmother sighed, went back to stitching. Her knuckles were sore. The thread that had once bound her House to her back kept coming undone with small *pings,* like broken guitar strings, hanging loose from the knobs of her spine. Only recently had she discovered that she wasn't as frantic as she used to be to stitch herself back together again.

Porous

It didn't take long for Mother to discover where Father had gone. In no time, dinner invitations scattered the woods like a trail of bread crumbs across fragile leaves. Mother peered through the foliage at the edge of the Hollow, wearing a faded white floral dress that clung to thick hips still wet from the dishes. The tip of her nose was as far as she ever ventured into the woods. She fidgeted awkwardly at the border, waiting until Father came to see her.

After many hours the Wild Thing would finally lope out of the Hollow. He'd rub his mangy fur over her prickly legs, leaning his bone-and-wolf body against her thighs, and Mother would close her eyes and let out a tiny sigh.

Sometimes Father never came out to see her at all, ignoring her presence in his languor by the stream. But he always knew when he was wanted.

Implicit in these Hollow visits was a request: *come to dinner, sweetheart. Come to the girls' little production. They're doing Macbeth. Essie's talking enough now to play the witches. All three.* He'd shrug his Wild Thing shoulders as she pleaded with him, refuse to follow her. But eventually, as the afternoons grew old, Father padded his way from the Hollow to the place where he'd first met his wife. Even in his wolfish state the trip felt so ancient, so laden with nostalgia. It was more migration than visit.

What Miriam had begun could not be undone. Father faded. While the little girl had freed him from his suits and ties and polish, relinquished Father to fur and claws and fangs, the Hollow wasn't satisfied. Material comforts weren't sacrifice enough: Wildness had to rule. Soon time was stolen from him too. Time like the hours in the morning when you feel most alive, or the seconds before you fall asleep and can almost imagine that you're floating, or those rare periods when you find yourself completely and peacefully alone. His arrival in the Hollow rendered each precious moment obsolete.

Speech was next. At first the only phrases missing were *it'd be my pleasure* and *as you wish*. But that was just the start: in no time *certainly*, *clearly*, *of course* and *definitely* disappeared too. After those first casualties Father lost language in a landslide of consonants and vowels—*hunger*, *heaping*, *hubris*. Only out of fierce determination was he able to keep *I love you* and *sweet dreams*. Deep down he knew their days were numbered too.

Even as moments and language grew extinct within him, one second, one letter at a time, some things couldn't be siphoned. Not even from a Wild Thing. So when Mother invited him to dinner he felt compelled to attend. But like every displaced being, he made the trips to his family's House hunting for an ecosystem that was already lost. The place he searched for could never be found and yet it still called to him with primordial cries.

On each trip it was necessary for the wolf to avoid his family's sentinel: Grandmother always sat at the cookfire in front of House. Ever since Grandfather died and his key with him, Grandmother had to work with her House still fused to her back. There, in the wavering flames, she cut off old, shrunken fabric and grafted the severed pieces together. Despite the absence of a second half, she was forever tightening ship.

The old woman didn't see the black, matted wolf sneaking behind her House, padding his way to the makeshift window of glass so old that, if you looked closely, you could see the sand still trapped inside. The window was wide and many-paned, recycled over generations. Father pressed his pink, peeling nose to the glass.

If it was possible, the remains of House on Mother's back looked even larger than the day he'd left. They hung in haphazard chunks of metal, washboards, melted crayons. House clung to her shoulders like a child afraid of slipping off, and Mother leaned forward as if she too felt the burden of gravity.

Each time the Wild Thing came for dinner—the clandestine creature on the other side of the glass—the girls would sit with empty plates before them for hours on end. They wore white dresses with lavender bows. Both girls seemed to have lost their shoes and they swung their bare feet, played toe games, kicked one another's pudgy legs.

"Don't worry," Mother would say. "We can eat when he arrives." The girls would sit—hands neat, faces still, legs swinging—until their mother decided it was no use to wait. The food was getting cold anyway. After their bellies had been full for some time, Mother would say with a sigh that they might as well start their after-dinner show without Father. He must be delayed for some reason, caught up by something important. They could eat dessert after—Father wouldn't want to miss the cake. The girls would set up their playhouse by hanging a sheet across House that acted as a curtain between the mechanics of their magic and their tiny audience.

From the other side of the glass, Father would growl when Macbeth pushed a topsy-turvy, baby-faced Macduff to the ground. He would chuff at the little-girlish Macbeth laying down her cardboard sword, proclaiming, "and all our yesterdays have lighted fools the way to dusty death." Her words, her little child-anger, made his stomach sink. And so the Wild Thing grew uncomfortable in the world of words and wars and families. Eventually, before the show ended and dessert began, Father would always turn and drift away into the Hollow.

Father truly believed that someday Mother would stop her invitations, that someday he'd stop coming. But both Mother and Father had lost control of their mismatched compulsions, their inescapable seesaw. Unable to resist his family, Father would migrate to a window in the woods, drawn by the prehistoric call of this woman he loved in a place deeper than memory. Coming to dinner but never making it past the window became habitual, a life-history structured into his Hollow world. Father's obligatory march ended at this place he felt in his blood—in the humming recognition of the wound beneath his ribs—the dark side of a wide, paned window.

Petal-Stitch

Father still carried the shadows of House, its carcass like a phantom limb. The old bruises were still sensitive to touch. The Wild Thing was aggravated, even now, by his skeletal home. It took a crafty hand to move without feeling, to walk ahead ignoring the imaginary smell of mildew and cardboard rotting on his back.

The hole the key had left in his side pained him, and for his first few weeks in the Hollow, a pink gash remained in the soft flesh of his hip. It never healed completely, but occasionally the wound glossed over with yellow, sticky pus. It itched and burned, and it was never long before Father ripped the tear open again. Somehow along the way, seeds drifted from the forest above and made their way in the flesh of his wound.

It took two days for Father's side to blister and the seeds inside to flower on his skin. He cried out in agony as the roots burrowed into the sinews of his sides.

He remembered being told once, as a human, that he swallowed eight spiders a year. Out here, then, how many earwigs and darkling beetles trembled their many-legged-walk down his esophagus?

Around the time the seeds sprouted in his lungs, Father started coughing up pollen. He began falling asleep with the weight of a tiny, phantom body on his chest. Breathing was difficult, and often he gasped himself awake in search of the oxygen his lungs could no longer hold. After several months in the Hollow, one of the seeds planted inside his body germinated into a tiny tree.

The tree intertwined with the veins, organs and muscles of his abdomen. At its core were Father's lungs. He struggled to get comfortable as he fell asleep every day. Branches protruded so that he couldn't sleep on his side; instead he had to lie with his pink belly and black nipples facing up. Even the slight weight of a centipede crawling across his stomach awakened him. All night long he coughed. The roots of the tree clenched his lungs tighter and tighter; he could feel them like fingernails digging into his lungs with every breath.

Every night, as Father fell into the limbo between dreams and consciousness, the Hollow made itself known. The place surged into his mind with arrogant power as a single drumbeat reverberating through his core, reminding him that it was simply another cage for Wild Things without names.

Battening

Miriam came home from playing in the woods to find House filled with steam. Years later, the smell of lavender at twilight would still unleash a flood within her. Unbidden, she'd recall images of water hanging suspended above stone, ready to seep into the earth below.

Miriam tucked her head into the bedroom, behind the cloud of hanging blankets and the wall of worn, holey flannel to where her mother lay, eyes closed.

"Hello?"

"Come in, sweetie."

Mother held her own nakedness to her chest. A huge emptiness lay beside her.

"Come here." Mother reached out and the little girl crawled into the blankets, aware that there was dirt in her ears, mud below her nails. The rest of the world seemed cool and light against Mother's body, still hot from the bath, her breath clammy on Miriam's neck. She wriggled away but Mother pawed her closer.

"Just for a second, sweetie. You girls grow up so fast."

"I'm not grown up yet." But she let Mother wrap soft arms around her, gently kiss her neck. When Mother's lips pressed against her skin, ripples of sadness leaked from somewhere deep inside her. Sadness raised the hairs on the little girl's skin.

I wish you wouldn't kiss me like that, Miriam wanted to say, but Mother pulled the little girl tight to her breasts, her chest rocking with every breath. Mother's movements slowed; soon she would sleep. So Miriam said nothing at all. She felt her skin shrink against her bones. She counted her heartbeats.

It will be over soon, Miriam thought, wishing she were more generous, that she weren't the kind of daughter who felt sadness skate below her flesh at the touch of her Mother's lips. That she weren't the kind of daughter who felt caught, like a rabbit in a trap, whenever Mother wrapped warm arms around her hips, tugged her close.

It wasn't just Mother who made her feel slick and blue. Miriam knew this. The howls of the Wild Things brought her that wet sadness too. Her whole life, whenever sadness had gotten the best of her, it had filled her chest with phlegmy fluid and made her sick. She always coughed it out in hard green rocks or slimy yellow slugs. It was hard to move when she felt so full. Sometimes it took days for Miriam to drain herself dry again.

If only she could catch the sadness fast enough. Dike the sea.

After Father had left, Miriam had discovered that she had a plug of her own. The magic was this: all she had to do was slip it inside to listen to the moan and hunt of the Wild Things. There was no leak. Only the rush in the back of her throat, the gasp of her voice waiting to be let free.

Tonight Miriam knew what had happened: the sound of the Wild Things was too near and Mother hadn't yet discovered her own plug. Miriam wondered if Mother was too old to begin the search. But what if it was possible for Mothers to grow so wet they drowned from the inside? The bathtub within Mother was not something Miriam could watch over.

A long, guttural howl bellowed through the fabric shards that shielded them from the night, and Mother shivered uncontrollably. Miriam listened to the howl the way she looked at her Mother's face: inspecting her cheekbones, her chin, trying to find a Miriam inside Mother, a Mother inside Miriam. The low call floated away. *Is that what I sound like? Is that what I come from?*

"Mother?" Miriam asked.

"Hm?"

"What if I'm not worth it?"

Mother's leg twitched; her eyelashes fluttered against Miriam's neck.

"Worth what, sweetie?"

"Never mind." She closed her eyes. Let herself fall asleep in Mother's arms.

Retaining Wall

Even children have questions they are frightened will go unanswered forever. Who better than little girls to go searching for stories to tell in the dark? Miriam had grown tired of her Mother's invitations, her father's stunted migration, and so she grabbed baby Essie's fingers. "Let's go hunting," she said. Essie sucked on her lips in agreement.

It wasn't difficult to find the Hollow in the woods: Miriam just followed her nose. As the trees grew denser and the rivulets congealed into brooks, the smell grew. The miasma of the Hollow was rank and soft; you could slice the air into thick pieces. Carrion was the most wretched odor of them all, she decided. It smelled of rejection and leftovers.

Essie held her nose and breathed only through her mouth, but Miriam let the pungent stench fill her lungs. *One, two, three, four*—she grew large with the smell. It was a game of tolerance. How much decay could she stomach?

Soon the howls began. Mournful and wrenching, the sound filled the woods. Miriam walked faster, nostrils stinging and ears ringing.

It was hard to say the origin of the compulsion that drew her to the Hollow. But if Miriam had truly understood why she followed the smell of rotting corpses, the sound of the Wild Things, she'd have turned around. She'd have run. She'd have never taken baby Essie hunting again.

The woods opened for them and the girls found themselves standing on the precipice of the Hollow. Below, hundreds of Wild Things bathed in the water, the sludge and waste.

"Don't be afraid," Miriam said, and she and her sister ran down the hill.

Miriam searched for her father's face among the Wild Things. Perhaps that was his nose in the snout she saw? Were those his eyes? As the children picked their way between bodies, the Wild Things growled. Yellow eyes narrowed to nothing. The animals parted their thick black lips, revealing pink gums and shiny teeth. Tongues slid over incisors, licking with intention.

Just look forward.

At the center of the Hollow was a commotion. Furred bodies piled over one another until she couldn't distinguish one animal from its brother. Miriam froze when she came to the edge of the tangle of flesh and fur. Drawn by something within her history, something without a name, compelled to find Father somewhere among the Wildness, Miriam dragged baby Essie towards the mass of animals. She could hear the gnash of teeth, threatening snarls, yips of terror.

Just look forward.

And there he was. Masticating on the haunch of elk, Father looked up to see his little girls in their white dresses and muddy shoes. A tree grew from a gaping wound at his side. Seeing him, so close and so real after all these months, made Miriam's stomach release. She felt herself get sick, and as she doubled over she watched Father watch them.

Raw intestines curled from between his lips, and distantly Miriam wondered if he'd eaten the heart of the animal or if it had gone to some other Wild Thing. *What does meat taste like when it's still so fresh?* Without taking his eyes from her, Father slurped the entrails into his mouth, his jaw pumping. Blood stained his teeth. Baby Essie was crying, clinging to Miriam's leg.

Do you know me? Miriam asked him silently. All at once she realized that was all she wanted to understand. If she had to, she'd wait her whole life to hear the answer. *Do you still know me?*

The elk disappeared fast as each Wild Thing came to the cache and took something away. The beast was devoured, chunk by chunk, until only its fleshless carcass remained—femurs dragged away to places where they could be consumed in private, head separated from body, and still they remained hungry.

Father looked up from the bones into Miriam's eyes, lips puckered. At first Miriam thought it was a smile. But then the Wild Thing raised his hackles, stalked forward with all the confidence of a predator sure that he will outrun his prey. The tone of the rally shifted imperceptibly. Where moments before disappointment and dissatisfaction had ruled, there was now a palpable scent in the air. It filled the woods, released from the Wild Things themselves: expectation. As one, the pack turned to look at the children, hunger rumbling in its belly.

Miriam didn't take her eyes off of Father. She couldn't explain how she knew this Wild Thing, with the blackest eyes and a tree growing between his ribs, was her own. All she knew was that when she looked at him the string of her spirit vibrated in recognition. The way family, even transformed and unfamiliar, has the power to wring music from your bones.

Do you still know me?

Miriam grabbed her sister's hand and backed away from the animals, but the tighter Miriam squeezed the more Essie squirmed. "Let me go."

"Stay here." Miriam felt her arm grow slack at the socket—it was getting harder to hold her sister close.

"Let me *go*." Baby Essie jolted away from her sister and into the hungering crowd.

Something dark and thick grabbed hold of Miriam as she watched her little sister plunge forward into the bloody heat of the Wild Things. As frightened as she was, she couldn't help but marvel as she watched Essie walk into the gathering, head up, eyes forward, both hands outstretched in a silent offering to the pack. Wild Things closed in around her.

"Essie, come back!" She could no longer see her sister inside the mass of fur and slender haunches.

A muted, deep growl grew from the animals in a heavy hum. Their snarl stretched louder and wider, swallowing the sound of Miriam's heartbeat, her breath.

"It's okay. I won't bite." Essie's voice rose from within the circle.

A Wild Thing gnashed his teeth.

Don't be afraid.

Miriam forced her body through the sea of wolves, lunging for baby Essie. *At least I'll go first,* she thought. *Maybe one will be enough.* With a snap, the nearest Wild Thing clamped onto Miriam's ankle. It was an exploratory bite, almost playful, barely drawing blood, but all the same Father zeroed in. She could feel his breath, still wet from the blood of the elk, on her skin. Right before his mouth closed around her calf, Father smiled wide. His bite created teeth-sliding-into-girl sounds.

As soon as he tasted her, salt on his lips, Father let go. Her blood still on his tongue, her skin stuck between his teeth, Father let out a howl and the Hollow seethed in response. Beasts fumed and pawed the ground. Father had offered more food, only to take it away. A promise had been broken. He turned to face his pack—teeth bared, body solid between children and beasts. As if released from a spell, Miriam swooped baby Essie into her arms, turned and ran.

Once both girls were safely back in House, Miriam couldn't stop touching Essie's arms, her toes, her ears.

Are you hurt?

I'msosorry

I'msosorry

I'msosorry

Pleaseforgiveme

It'sallmyfaultit'salwaysmyfaultitwillalwaysbemy faultIwillneverloveyouenough

"Don't be sad," Essie said. But tears streamed down her face, too. "Don't be sorry."

It'snotourfault

It'snotourfault

Itwasneverourfault

Look, you're bleeding.

Miriam's calf throbbed. She bent over and discovered a chunk of her flesh was missing. Father had left a Moon-shaped hole in her.

Spalling

Miriam was by the inside fire, the one they only used in the winter for heat, when a black wolf peered through the tarnished window. The Wild Thing scratched at the glass, whining under his breath.

It was one of those winter afternoons where to look outside is to lose yourself. Centuries ago, in a different world and a different time, on her family's farm, Miriam's ancestors—closer to cavemen than housebearers —had tied a tether from the barn to the farmhouse during a blizzard. They'd held onto the string as they walked to feed the animals, feeling the tough hemp between their fingers. Only white had surrounded them. On those days, like space or open water, they'd walked next to a tightrope. Snow days were worlds without bottoms or boundaries.

For Miriam and the women of her family, waiting was blood-born. Miriam could stand at the window staring out at the swirling white for days and never sense the claustrophobic twinge in her chest most people feel when looking at things that have no end.

She raised her head at the sound of his scratching, set down her thread and pressed her nose to the window. There they stood for several moments, nose to muzzle, fog obscuring everything but their eyes. The Moon-shaped hole in her calf stung. Pain spread up her leg. Terror and joy swelled within her.

Do you still know me?

She let the animal through the front door. Putting a finger to her lips, she said, "Mother's at work, Essie is with Grandmother. I'm all alone."

All these months, Miriam had always known when her father came to the window. Sometimes she'd look up from her stitching to his smooth pelt, his bright teeth. But when Father arrived that night, shivering in the middle of a snowstorm that shielded the whole world, she didn't ask him why he'd never before come in from outside, why he always watched their plays through the window and disappeared before the curtain closed. And Father didn't tell her how the cold perforated his bones— that the weight of his skeleton was no more than hers.

"You can't stay long." Miriam said.

Father ignored her and slid towards the fire. His black body a slit in space.

Thousands of years ago whales and wolves were one and the same. How do we know this? Because whale spines undulate through the waves as they swim, and wolves run in waves too, their backs controlling the rolling motion of their legs—a fin slicing its way through thick water. Father carried that ancestor within the coding of his cells. He moved like a whale to the fire. The melting snowflakes flowed off of his bony back in small tides.

Miriam sat next to him, criss-cross-applesauce. Father's body wracked as he coughed; pollen spat from his mouth and sprayed against the ground.

"It's okay, Dad." Miriam said. She smoothed her apron and he lay his head in her lap. "It's going to be okay." The smell of him made her throat swell, redolent of an apartment left alone too long—sweaty, smoky furniture, dampness and rot. His hair was falling out in patches, revealing blue skin with brown spots. The ribs of his tight animal body cut into her knees. He breathed in and out with hot, sick breath, his snout twitching. He still had the hole she'd left in his side; the stitches had come undone and from his wound a tiny tree had sprouted. It punctured through the surface of his skin. Miriam could see through his muscle and into his lungs.

How beautiful, she thought. Such blue skin, such black hair and green leaves.

"I tell you, I am dying," he said, rubbing his forepaws against the wound. She could tell he wanted to say more, but he was having trouble opening his mouth and releasing words. Garbled barks and consonants tumbled out.

Miriam closed her hands about the branch protruding from him and began to tug. He let out a low growl and bit her. Blood pooled on her wrist between his teeth.

"All right." Miriam shrugged and let go of the little branch. "You smell," she told Father, scrunching her nose.

The wolf nodded. "I tell you, I am dying," he repeated.

"So you said." She ran her hands over his brow-bone, snout, ear.

"I've always loved you, you know," Father said, turning to face the fire. "Since the moment you were born, all blue and red." His words came out slowly. This was the last of it—speech withered in his chest and sank there. Each word became a treasure chest he'd sailed oceans to unearth. Yet Father had discovered too late there wasn't as much treasure as he remembered. It wasn't enough. There was never enough.

"So you said."

Miriam looked at him and understood: he'd said all he could. But inside there was an unnamable grief. There are never the right words. She knew this. But she'd never even hear her Father come close.

"It's all right, Father." Miriam kissed his sunken cheek. "I'll sing this time."

tears weave—don't leave me now
pinned between wing and earth
carry me free, I don't have legs to stand
I am heavy, heavier than your dreams

Oh, the lies that daughters tell....

Seam Ripper

But little girls are rarely good at stitching. Often they leave pieces behind, and even Wild Things have to learn to care for their remains.

"You are not dying, Father," Miriam said, once she'd finished the song. "You are leaving."

"I tell you, I am dying."

"And I tell you, you're already dead."

"A dead man can die twice. Tell me you love me."

"You can't help but love a Wild Thing. When you are wild you get away with everything."

"Have I told you that I've always loved you?" Father said.

"Yes, you've told me."

A murky green tear dripped down his black cheek. "Good. As long as you know," he said. Several more goopy, sick tears followed the first. "As long as you know I mean it."

"You have to go back," the little girl said.

The Wild Thing let out a slow, guttural moan. His body shuddered.

"You can't be two things at once, you know." Miriam whispered. "That's not the way this works."

"But what about two places at once?"

"Maybe. I don't think there are rules for that. No one can tell you where to go in your heart."

Miriam let him sleep for a little while. After an hour or so she blew into Father's ear just the way he'd done to her when she was little.

"Rise and shine, it's a new day," she whispered. "I don't want Mother to see you here."

He looked up at her with empty, black-plate eyes.

She pulled on her boots, black coat and black hat with the tassel on the top. Father had laboriously risen and was standing in the doorway.

"Come," she said, and walked outside. Father followed. The two of them slipped into the woods. No one could distinctly see past their nose; no one could determine what was sky and what was earth. But if anyone had looked outside, they would have seen a black wolf walking next to a little girl in a black coat, all the way to the end of their vision. The little girl walked with her Wild Thing further than she'd ever walked before.

Retaining Wall

"I tell you, I am dying," the wolf said when they had reached the end.

"And I tell you—you are not. Not now. Not yet." She touched the creature on his cheek. "The you you once were died a long time ago. Now you're just beginning." She looked down. "I'm not allowed to walk past this clearing,"

"I understand." He slid his caged body against his daughter's leg and let out a tiny whine.

The Wild Thing paused for a moment to look back at her and then ran off—a black whale-wolf swimming through the white, white night.

Warp Threads

From the edge of the woods Miriam could see the light of her Mother's cook-fire. She could taste smoke on her tongue. Smolder and snow melded together to create the sensation of liquid fire sticking to her cheeks, running down her eyelashes. She wasn't ready to come home so instead she hung below the branches of pines, lingering in the woods a little while longer. There she was: a tiny animal concealed by her black coat, her still body and the night growing thick around her.

Mother squatted over the stew. It was a marvel she didn't fall over, sitting like that at the edge of the flames. Quite suddenly she looked up into the woods and said, "there you are. Come on out."

"How did you know I was here?" Miriam stepped out of the forest and into the firelight, hoping she didn't smell of sweat and Wild Things.

"I could see your eyes."

"I could've been a deer. Or a bear," Miriam said.

"But you're not."

"Did you know that nocturnal animals have a layer of reflective cells called *tapetum lucidum* across their eyes?"

"Oh?"

"So when light hits, it strikes twice. That's why foxes' eyes shine."

"How interesting," Mother said, stirring the stew. Steam lifted upwards through her hair, hung around her face like a cloud over a mountain peak. "Where did you learn that?"

"Dad told me."

Mother stopped stirring, looked up at Miriam and the sky behind her. "What about me? Do you remember anything I tell you?"

Miriam closed her lips. The light of the fire grew smaller and smaller; Mother hadn't gathered enough kindling. She'd put the logs on too quickly, like always. Twigs used up too soon and now there were only embers. Miriam turned, began to search the forest's edge for any wood that had survived the snow and the dark night. Wet wood makes for a sad fire.

"Of course you don't," Mother said.

"I don't need to," Miriam whispered. Hunting for the perfect branches to stoke the flames.

"What did you say?"

People say that snow falling to earth sounds like peace, or joy, or a gasp of relief. But that isn't true. Snow hitting the ground makes no sound. *Why make something out of nothing?* Miriam wondered. Here she was, standing with her Mother at the edge of the woods during a snowstorm, and it was silent.

"I said I don't need to. Remember anything you tell me." Already Miriam held an armful of kindling—it wasn't hard to find the dry wood. Her mother was always in such a hurry to get cooking. Never bending below the bushes to find the good stuff.

"Am I so uninteresting to you?" Mother was still crouched around the pit, coiled and hard, the light making her lean body sharper. *She sits like an animal,* Miriam thought, watching Mother rock from thigh to thigh. Feet as muscled paws, ready to spring up in an instant. *I've never even looked at her teeth,* Miriam realized.

The little girl put her bushel of sticks beside the pot, making sure she didn't touch her mother's fingers or palms. Forever making sure to leave Mother her space by the fire.

"I don't need to remember because you're right here. I can just ask you again."

Mother picked up one of the sticks and twirled it between her gloved fingers. Nothing spoke. Even the trees leaned away from the woman and the girl huddled in snow. Waning firelight shimmered across Mother's face; it looked to Miriam as if her Mother was trapped below a river or a well. Above the clearing the Bony Moon hung distended and fair. Bony Moon. Here to remind them that this was a season where not only animals died. Miriam watched Mother's tiny fingers spinning the stick, the graceful way her neck seemed to always cradle her head, her shoulders strong enough to bear any weight. She looked at Mother and felt herself filling up, growing wet and wide. Soon there would be no space left and all her air would be forced out. But Miriam dug in her heels. She let the sea rise. She'd float if she had to.

"Did you know, Mother, that when I look at you, I see only water?"

"Well, at least you see something," Mother said tightly. "Dinner will be ready soon. Essie is inside. Why don't you help with the bath?"

Miriam nodded and walked towards House. She looked behind her just long enough to watch Mother place the kindling below the pot. Dry needles spat into flame. The logs ignited.

Caulking

Miriam poured the final pot of water into the bath. Watched as the steam rose in threads of silver and unspooled into the cold night air.

"Is it too hot?"

Essie shook her head and Miriam slipped first her toes, then her shins, then her bare chest below the water. There was barely enough room for two bodies between the stones, so both girls washed their feet and elbows without knowing which limb belonged to which sister.

"Are you ready?" Miriam asked when their hair was washed, their ears clean.

"Yes." Essie's green eyes blinked back at her sister, wet and open.

Both girls reached out and plugged the other's nose. They were eye-to-eye, body-to-body.

"One. Two. Three."

Together the sisters plunged below the water. Around them the stones of their grandmother's bathtub smoothed slick and black against their skin.

They knew that water was more powerful than everything. It was larger than their voices, their heaviness. And so, when the little girls opened their mouths and screamed, there was not a soul that could hear them. Their sounds were for them and them alone. Together they put their hands to each other's chests. They felt their bodies speak, the water take it all away. Hair flew around them in dark waves.

Neither girl had to say *I'll always be with you* or *you don't have to be afraid of the water* or *we'll take care of each other*—the sea knew. The sea knew and she let their words run through her.

Acknowledgements

Firstly, I'd like to thank my mother. This book, my life, would not be possible if not for your unwavering love. Thank you for allowing me my own story and your patience while I begin to understand yours. And Frank— what would life be if not for you? I thank the magic of this world that you were born and I got the privilege of being your sister. And Tangy—we all came from you and you are a real human hero.

These pages would still be in the bottom of a college bin if not for the thoughtful and tender care of Kaisa Cummings. Thank you for reading this book what feels like twenty times without complaint. Your friendship brought poetry back into my life. I will forever remember the Alaskan light in your kitchen, feeling something frigid within begin to thaw.

I'd still be creatively caged if not for Josh Corey, who forced me to look beyond the glass of poetry. The genesis of this project began in his classroom. And for Monica Sparks, you taught me to ask "what does it mean to be human?". Even if I might never find the answer, it is in the question. I'd nearly given up on this project before taking Mark Mayer's class and I might never have found footing here if not for his challenging questions and advice. And, of course, the Lighthouse—thank you for investing in me and our community.

To Daria, you've been a stalwart champion. I'm the Frodo to your Sam. I'd never make it Mount Doom without you. Joanna, you've helped me leap when I'm scared the next hold won't save me from a fall. Huan, your creative vision has inspired me more than you know. Jess, you appeared during a dark time and have been nothing but light.

Special thanks to Topaz Winters and Danie Shokoohie for all your efforts and the tender yet fierce lens through which you see the world. Thank you for your work in promoting unique voices.

To Sheila, who brought unspeakably beautiful magic into my life and to whom I will always be incredibly thankful.

For Anna— you've helped me to see that I need not be housebearer or wild thing. There's a whole beautiful world in between. I've never felt so full of possibility as I do with you. You have all my love, unbound.

And finally, this book is for you, Dad. Perhaps somehow, impossibly, you can read these words and know I will always love you. I hope you are wild and free.

About the Author

The poet Ed Roberson once told Sammie Downing, "You only have one life and you only have one work." She's taken this advice perhaps too literally and has lived in 7 states and two countries. She's been a housekeeper, a huntress and a fraud investigator. Currently, she resides in Denver, Colorado. She looks forward to her next adventure.

Printed in the USA
CPSIA information can be obtained
at www.ICGtesting.com
LVHW050230151223
766573LV00045B/1173